The Isodora –
A Christmas Tale

The Isodora –
A Christmas Tale

Clarence Silvers

ISBN: 979-8-9861052-0-8

The Colonial Period in the Northern Hemisphere French Louisiana 1702 to 1763

Background

The coastal lands that were not the Americas remain small coastal communities. Some were 300 to 400 in population. It took some time to develop into bustling township. Most of the people lived off the land. They were farmers, builders, merchants, hunters, and troopers. At the time, these remote places depended on the merchant ships for everyday supplies. As many areas grew, the need to develop the land grew. More crops, more houses, and more roads were needed to accommodate the masses. Many areas in the 1700's had a need for workers and cheap laborers to do the hard work. Regions in the northern hemisphere turn to slavery to meet this need. In 1721 the Africans sailed into Mobile Harbor with a cargo of over 100 slaves. In 1724 the French Code Noir or The Black Code extended from the French West Indies to North American colonies institutionalizing slavery in the Mobile area.

Introduction

This story is based on the experience aboard and beyond the Isadora. Captain Jonathan Parker, his crew members, and three slaves; during the period of the French Colonies; experienced a common but unusual change of heart in the treatment of enslaved people of Africa; pilgrimaging to the Americas. It is a story to remember. DHD

The Isadora –
A Christmas Tale

CAPTAIN JONATHAN PARKER came from a long line of family members who were sailors. His grandfather and father had been commanders. He was 54 years old, and had spent his life on the ocean. Captain Parker loved the ocean, but it had cost him dearly. He had no family or knew of no relatives in the whole world that he could call his family. His mother, father, and brother had long since died, so he was all alone. He sat quietly in his cabin looking at the four walls thinking about his past, his not so distant future and what would happen to him if he could live on the ocean forever. In time he would have to go ashore to live; to retire from the sea and become a land-lover; something he did not take likely. He thought he might go to the family farm which had been deserted almost eight years since the last surviving relative lived there. It could be home again; with a little work he thought to himself. A dreadful feeling came over him as he contemplate on giving up the Sea; his home for more than forty years; and the only true home he knew. His crew, his family; Daniel and Harmon had been like bothers to him. What would he do on land without his sea family? How would he live?

In an instant, the ship began to rock from side to side and then the vessel appear to dive nose first down in a valley of water on all sides as if it had been swallowed up. Down it went. After a while, it rose again to an even keel and leveled off for a few minutes and the hold process started over again. By now the captain had made his way to the cabin door and up the stairs. As he stood looking at the helmsman drenched in the cold salt water; he could see with each pounding wave the ship responded well to the rough treatment; which now covered the ship's deck. He was satisfied with the helmsman's ability to control the situation.

The old captain still had not come up with a true plan for his future. Looking somewhat puzzle, he moved about the deck checking sails, rigging, and mask for signs of trouble. He greeted members of the crew who were on duty with a nod. In his mind he muddles over the deal he had made with the American, and the money Mr. Matthew Collins had already paid him for his first two loads of captives. There were 200 for each trip which total four hundred dollars. Two hundred were due on December 24, 1815 at the harbor in Mobile, Alabama. A deal had been made, and there was no backing out now. It was $1,000 now and $2,500 on delivery plus the $200 dollars per crew member, and the last expected sale of the Isadora for $1,700 dollars. Money had been spent to redesign the hauling to accommodate the new cargo the ship would be hailing to make way for at least two hundred captives on each voyage to America. The vessel had extra platforms which would be used as a living space along with an area for more supplies, such as food and water for the human cargo's long trip which could take from 30 to 45 days in good weather. The captain finished his rounds and return to his cabin. He took a seat in his chair at his desk. He took out his long book and added today's notes.

In a matter of two and a half days, he would arrive onto the Barry Coast of Africa where he would see the slaves and collect his cargo. Till now the hunt for humans had remain pretty much on the coastal areas raiding small villages there, but the black skin people were getting harder and harder to find, plus, there was a resistance move against the slavers. Armed freedom fighters were springing up to save their people from the non-country men now that they knew the captured would never return home once in the clutches of the hunters. So inland was the next choice for the radar to get unsuspecting captives, as no one knew of their activities. They would be vulnerable to the tasks of capture and the long forced march to the prison camps on the coastal sights; boarding the many slave ships awaiting their arrival. The jungle prison sight was known to a few of the lead slavers which help to prevent escape. Upon the arrival of the Isadora, around 50 blacks had been brought into the capture sight. This was just the third day the trapping team of 10 to 15 men had been out collecting. Today they moved in deeper in the forest area well in from the coastline base of operations. Some of the tribes only numbered 30 to 40 members total, so if a fight broke out, they would be able to suppress the resistance easily, but it would take longer to locate and capture; not like some of the larger tribes numbering well over 100 to 200 in size, some even larger than that with 60 to 70 warriors armed and ready to fight intruders. The plan was to always stick to the small villages.

It was a pleasant day in the African bush country where two women and a small boy made their way to a nearby watering hole which they had done a hundred times before. They gathered the water supply for the day. Each day someone from the many families in the village made their pilgrimage to the only available water source for the day which would be used for drinking and cooking. The sun had just started to rise as the three villagers made their way down the man-made trail pushing back the large bushes that align each side of the path. The winding foot path made its way down a small grade and then started up again disappearing in the bush once more. The three figures continued forward until finally reaching the bank that surround the standing water.

The land around the water hole had been cleared back about 20 o 25 feet for safety purposes. Large predatory animals also visited this spot for water, but most of the time it was safe for nearby villages to come. Each of the women had a large clay pot which they carried on their head when it was fill with water, and the young male child carried a spear for protection to ward off animals and man alike. Soon the water hole would be visited by other villages. By getting there earlier, the two women and the boy would put themselves ahead of the crowd. On the opposite shore a few birds and monkeys were there taking their fill of the fresh water for the day. When the animals observed the humans they quickly moved off in the high brush, or in the air out of reach.

The two women began filling the jugs as the boy kept watch. The party of huntsmen had left the coast working their way inland in the hopes of raiding small unsuspecting villages. Their trip was a full day's march through bush country which would take almost a day and a half to reach any settlements.

Most of their success up till now was catching natives who were separated from the main body of people from their village which would be some in the fields, small hunting parties, or strays who could be captured easily. This time their march would bring them in range of several watering holes and farm fields in which the villages depended on for food, for livestock, and for themselves. The twenty men had travel all day and a night. It was early morning when they took position in their hiding spot; concealing themselves in the high grasses waiting for their first victim. The day was progressing on. It was now 8:00am, but no sign of anyone. To maximize their efforts, the party divided into four groups of five men at the watering holes, so that the day would not be a lost. Each sight was under surveillance.

Just like clockwork, the three people who appeared were the two women and the boy coming down the partially covered trail to the water sight. The men kept silent and well hidden as the unsuspecting natives moved closer to the trap. First the boy had to be disarmed before captured. The two men would see to that while the other three men held the women at bay. Minutes passed as the five men observed their soon to be prisoners. The two huntsmen swung into action taking the young boy down by force, pending him to the ground, and relieving him of his weapon. Seconds later, the women saw the danger and began to run towards the safety of the villages, but they were soon cut off from their retreat; surrounded by three men and their weapons that were ready to use them if necessary.

Now they were prisoners being hurled off somewhere away from home; the land they knew in the early morning; with no witnesses or help to rescue them from the present danger they were in. There would be no one to tell what had happen to them. Four teams had been dispatched in the hunt, and twenty five men, women and children had been captured and now on their way to the coast line of Africa where the waiting ships would start their long voyages across the oceans to distant lands. Some of the captives were able to communicate to others captives because they were locals and being neighbors of the area of their incarceration, but others could not. They were captives with no way of knowing what was happening to them and how their life would change. They would remain captives and sold to the highest bidder at the auction block.

Slaves had no rights. Some saw them to be less than human, and they would never see home again. The twenty five captives had been on a forced march for the coast with no rest, water, or food. They were held together with chains and whip to bend their will to the huntsmen who now drove the black prisoners. The sun had set, but the party of captives moved on all through the night reaching their destination. At 10:30 am the next morning; all of the prisons were in pins and kept there with armed guards just off the shore. Three large ships lay anchored in the deep waters. A cargo of slaves would be loaded in time to stay ahead of the going tide.

The Isadora was one of the ships off shore. Captain Parker had arrived some hours before sunrise. He sat quietly in his quarters as his men prepared the ship for its evening departure at 6:30 p.m. It would take a good part of the day to get supplies loaded and the count of 200 captives boarding the Isadora. Food and water was brought onboard for at least a 30 to 45 day voyage if no bad weather delayed the trip between continents. The seas could be unpredictable this time of year with constant storms. Captain Jonathan Parker sat at his desk completing his paper work. He had sailed from Great Britain to the West Indies and then to South Africa. The modifications to the Isadora had taken three weeks to complete. But, all was ready now; extra supplies were in place along with medical supplies. The seas appeared calm, but how long would this last. Winter storms manifest without warnings this time of year, and the months October and November is the start of ruthless weather.

The ship and its crew would have to ride out the storms as they manifest to get home safely. At this point, the last group of captives would arrive sometime late that day and then the process to assign them would begin. Finally, the loading would take place. The captain waited; hoping the weather would hold up, as it gave him the exit he needed to take to the open sea on voyage to the Americas to reach the Collins Plantation. The plantation was an eight hour march for the captive's new home; by wagon or horseback, but for waterlogged slaves who had hardly walked in thirty days, it would take longer. All was clear in the captain's mind on what was to be done to get paid. He thought hard to himself. "Just deliver the slaves;" slaves was not a term he easily used; it sort of stuck in his throat just to say it. But he was now a slave merchant like the men he once hated for the things they did for money. December 24th was the due date. He walked over to the small window of the vessel, looked out over the ocean and then made his way across the room to a cabinet located in a corner. He opened the cabinet door and took out a dark glass bottle which he then poured himself a drink. He returned to his chair and began looking over his daily log. Three o'clock p.m. November 4th. a) 21 barrels of water, b) 8 barrels of apples, c) 15 barrels of potatoes, d) 10 barrels of onions, dried salted fish and etc.

The group of captives from the South-West Bush country had numbered about 22 including a young male child, his mother and a neighbor who had been picked up through the night at a watering hold near their village. One person had been carried off by a big cat that had entered the camp undetected by the guards; which is common in the high bush country of Africa. No one fired a shot in hopes of not giving away their position in case someone was following the pack. So far, a brief rest was all they got and the pack was off again. Each prisoner wore a chain around a leg to assure there would be no escape. There were two men position on each side and in the front caring weapons and ready to use if the need arose.

It was 11:a.m. when the hunting party and their captives reached the coastal shoreline. It would take another hour and a half to get to the camp sight. Upon reaching the destination, the captives were placed in a holding area for inspection. Later they were separated into preselected groups for future shipment to their final destinations. The departure time grew closer. The captives had already started to load on the Isadora. When the count had been completed, the ship would set out to sea. Captain Parker finished his cup of ale and retired waiting to be notified of when to sail. As he lay quietly, he drifted into a dream state. For a while, the images related to pass events of his life. Some thoughts were pleasant, others he wished not to recall; but could not help himself. And so it was, he witness past events and present events in the dark places of his mind; black faces, hunting faces, thousands of faces wherever his mind took him. They were his new cargo, his new life line to a future on land. He stood like a red wood tree high above his captives looking down at his prisoners. In this nightmare, his face held a stern cold glare and his voice was angry as he barked orders to his crew while the captives looked on. As he wondered back to reality, his body trembled. With his eyes closed and hands covering both ears, the captain spoke out loud. "This is not me!" "I would never treat a fellow human being this way." "I'm a good man and liked by all who know me." He lowered his head in shame. Inside of himself, he could hear a voice saying "You are a slave trader; you sell human flesh; you care nothing for who you have enslaved, and then the captain heard a laugh. In an instant, the captain awoke and set up in his bed. With a wild look in his eyes, he began to wipe the sweat from his forehead. His eyes search the room. He wondered who was there; who was judging him for the crimes he had committed, but there was no one; just him and his creator, alone.

It was time. Two hundred captives had been chosen for the trip to the Americas. Mobile Alabama would be the port of call. First mates-Harmon Rum 'dose and Mr. Herbert Ran 'doff was the sergeant of arms and several arm guards stood along the path which lead to the Isadora. Among the captives were the young African boy, his mother and a woman from the same village. All the captives had been chained to each other for about fifteen days, and now it was time for the group to make their way toward the coast line of Africa where ships awaited their arrival. The loading of the captives would sometimes be escorted in small boats manned by two oarsmen; for the process would control the time the Isadora would set sail; if all was ready in time for high tide. But for now the weather posed no problem.

Even though storm season had started, the seafaring men look forward to put to sea to avoid bad weather. At 6:30 p.m. the coast line of Africa was far behind the sailing vessel. It's cargo of slaves would never see the Black Continent again. They were bound for the new world. For maximum capacity every available space had been filled with the black bodies below deck. The new design for the Isadora had worked. Thirty to forty days at sea would bring them to the coast of the new country. The hold of the ship was dimly lit, only the shadows of the human figures could be seen. The air was stale, unbearable, almost chocking to whoever breathe it, mounting each day, not counting the human waste pasted by people below deck. The young black boy and his mother worked in the galley and wherever else they were needed.

Rum 'dose spoke the language of most of the tribes and was able to translate the captain's orders and what was expected of them if they wanted to survive the ordeal. The captives belonged to the captain who was now their master, and in time they would be sold for profit. Do what you are told and remain safe was the bottom line. Other slave ships did not have anyone to translate for them. There were no communications except for the chains that help the white crew members keep order.

The Isadora had been put to sea; that night Rum 'dose and Mr. Ran 'doff made their rounds like they did many times before the voyage would come to an end off shore. As the two men made their way down through the hull of the ship, they could see the many bodies lying side by side with hardly enough room to walk without stepping on someone; from one end of the ship to the other. These duties were performed twice a day and the results reported to Captain Parker. Every cargo was money and could not be replaced; making the end product level lower. After the last round of the day, everyone had to be fed. Any server sickness was reported to the ship's doctor, Daniel Hopper; who also was the chapman and cook.

One small boy and two women were chosen to help in the task of feeding the captives, alone with six crew members. There were Strips of jerky, potato skins, bone parts, and some vegetables. They were placed in a mixture, a somewhat watered-down concoction, to stretch the portions to feed everyone. Sometimes the meal was a cup of water each day. Hardtack was added to the menu once a week. Many of the captives stayed sick throughout the voyage for lack of decent food, medical care, and being on board the ship which created motion sickness causing an inability to keep anything down. The first 10 to 12 days at sea following their illness, the captives began having bouts of severe diarrhea and abdominal pain.

The slaves came from many regions. Their dialects did not afford them ability to speak to each other which compound the situation of helplessness and confusion. Ever third day the captives were walked around the deck by crew members in order for the decks to be clean of debris and waste. This led to the breeding of germs, harmful to the cash cargo and the crew too. Ten days into the crossing, people had died making the total 192. The captain placed the lost to his log.

Daniel Hopper was everything. He was the cook, the chapman, and the medical provider for the ship. There were three slaves selected to help in the care of the captives. They were all given names; Black Jon, the young boy was named after Captain Jonathan Parker; Ruby was the name given to his mother because she wore a ruby colored scarf around her head; and Hoppy was the name given to the other women captured at the waterhole; she had a kind of hop in her walk. Mr. Hopper thought it was proper they be named since they worked so close to the crew in the daily task. Everything that had to be done for the black captives, they did it, and there was much to be done such as preparing the food and feeding them, cleaning up behind them; communication from Rum 'dose, and, even burial at sea. It was how the little freedom they had was earned. All three slept on the galley floor. They could witness firsthand how slaves were treated and how their masters lived and ate every day with no hopes or controls to change their life in the near future.

It was the 14th day at sea, 10:00 a.m. As Black Jon stood in the doorway of the galley looking out over the water which held him and his kind hostage; the gray clouds hung above the Isadora as she moved across the liquid surface which changed from second to second making its way toward the Americas. The sea would be rough sailing today. Jon looked intensely at the white caps which appeared and disappeared. There was no way to tell just where they were. The young boy knew nothing about the ocean and had never been to the shoreline of the country he was from. He only knew the jungle and the animals he saw every day. For miles it all looked the same, non-ending, only the moon and sun looked the same and gave some reference he could identify. A heavy heart griped Black Jon. With his head hung low, tears formed in his eyes which were consumed by the mist from the seawater which sprayed over the deck and all who was above deck.

The boy wiped his face clean of the water, but was soon covered again with salt water. The ship now was being tossed about. It moved up and down in the water, sometimes disappearing between walls of water before surfacing again. Minutes turned into hours with no change in the weather, the ship now faced a furious storm at sea. The gray sky formed its own wall of confinement, it was as if the vessel was enclosed in a fish bowl, and an outside force dictated the day's events. The storm raged on throughout the day, well into the night and early morning. The outcome could not be determined, for life and death could be decided here. This was the hazards of sailing on the open seas during storm season. Black Jon turned back toward the hole which was as dark as the night. A sound came from the darkness which he could not quite make, but he dare not go down there without permission. So he stood at the opening peering into the darkness.

He spoke in his native tongue and got no reply. The stillness below once more took over. Jon retreated towards the light taking a seat on a bag of potatoes which had been placed there to be used for the evening meal. Eyes were watching the boy which image somewhat blocked the light from the outside. As the ship pitched from side to side and up and down, the many bodies below deck swayed with each movement. The slave's uncontrollable fear could not find any form of satisfaction. The furious winds made its way down in the darkness. It was a numbing coldness with water covering the lower decks. Everything was wet. The smell of the wetness changed from a foul smell to a musty odor of rotting wood and whatever else mixed in with it. At some time the storm would come to an end, but the human misery would not. What would happen to the captives once they reached the land?

Another day began as the many faces below deck concentrated on the young boy's figure that stood in the doorway blocking the light which made its way through the opening and gave hope to the captives. The human smell now made its way to the top of the deck making some sick to their stomach and those below deck were over whelmed with agony. There was a combination of stomach fluids and feces covering the bodies below deck. Each third day the lower deck was cleaned by the deckhands including the young boy and the two women, but it was impossible for the crew to keep up with the cleaning task of almost two hundred passengers to ensure a healthy situation for all concern. Day and night were the same; no mercy was shown the captives, except when they were fed, or on the third day cleaning. The vessel plunged head first down in the cold water rising with its nose pointed to the sky every 3 or 4 seconds, rocking from side to side as its passengers lay on the cold wet wood. The bodies had developed sores, splinters and cuts from the floor they laid on.

The large, heavy chains also wore into the flesh of its captives zapping their strength when a line was raised. Most of the time, everyone laid quietly. The two-levels below had become rooms of pain and discomfort. The sounds of singing and moaning came from the hole permeating to the surface a deep sadness felt over and over by the captives. The sound could only be a gut wrenching reminder of what the loss of freedom was to all who heard or took part in the singing. Some of these words would later be known as Negro Spirituals. The spirituals kept the captives alive; hoping and trusting that they would survive the outcome. Happiness was far from this place, and heaven was just around the corner which many blacks would soon learn.

The old sailing vessel had seen many days which had turned into years on the oceans of the world. It stopped just long enough to repair her aging body from sea damage, and picked up a load of goods. It was a cargo bound to parts of the known world. The Isadora had weathered seas in good fashion, in bad weather, but now her age was starting to show. The deck, the mask, the siding had all been replaced many times and she still remain afloat. No matter what kind of face lift she got, her time like all things would come to an end. Her captain and crew had grown old on the sea. The salt water had taken its toll on all. The coming winter storms would prove to create a great burden on her; pulling at her from all directions, but it would sail on to their destination, the Americas; fighting her age old problems of decay, weakening side boards, which cause hull rotting throughout her body. High winds kept her nose low in the water one minute and pointing to the sky the next. Her decks washed with the acid like saltwater which weakened the metal and wood. The crew worked to keep a float each day.

As the new day began, the ocean horizon, like the sun, would not make an appearance due to the clouds and rain that covered the sky. The deck of the Isadora was drenched from the previous day and night of heavy rains. Only two deckhands were allowed on top of the deck, for fear of being washed over board was a high risk situation. The men on top took six hour shifts, and after ten minutes on deck, they were drenched by the sky water and the bitter salt water of the ocean. Temperatures stayed low, and present storms made it colder. The hands of the crew remain numb and recalled from the time spent in the extreme bad weather. The course was held as best they could with no sun or stars to steer by. Sometimes it varied and no course could be corrected till the good weather returned; for the compass was hampered by the movements of the ship in bad weather. The mask rigging swung loosely in the air with every movement of the ship.

The Devils House was the new name the Isadora took on; given to her by many ports she sailed from, such as the Americas, the Gold Coast, Senegal, Gambia, and Elmina. She also sailed to ports in Africa for the slave trade. Many people in the ports feared her and would stay clear of her or whispered to others about her when docked. The Isadora was a marked a slave ship. She joined the many other vessels that were slave vessels even though she was recorded as only making voyages from Africa to the Americas. She was a good sailing ship. The thick ropes that held and kept her sails in line looked like a large spider web woven to hold her prey, the slow moving current of air which made its way from bow to stern, the high platform for observation swayed from side to side with every movement of the vessel, A mist hovered just above the water's surface giving the impression that the surface did not exist. The side of the ship had been torn away; the covering rose high, and in time nothing above the deck could be seen. As the morning wore on, the mist and fog would give way to the heat of the day. It had been some time since the Isadora came cross any other ship in the shipping lane; not another living soul except its own crew, and this happen quite frequent.

Still in all, the Isadora moved forward ever so slowly to her destination. Crew members on watch, could be seen at their post in the worst of weather. The huge waves could be seen rising above the deck railing, spilling across the flat floor, wave after wave; crashing against the ship. The ship from the high winds change coarse even thou the helmsman fought to hold the ship on track.

Captain Parker had finished his morning inspection of his reports detailing the voyage up to date. The cargo hole had also been visited with the sergeant of arms and the medical officer to see just how well the human cargo was faring on the long trip to the Americas. Soon the Isadora would set in port off the coast of South America before making its way up to the warm waters of the gulf coast area. It was the last leg of the voyage before docking in Mobile, Alabama. The time had come when supplies were low from the many days at sea. Para, South America would be in range in a days' time and from that port San Domingo would be next then Mobile, Alabama; the last stop because of winter storms. In the Atlantic, travel would be slow; taking 2 to 3 weeks to navigate the rough waters. The open ocean of the voyage was over coastal shores and was in reach of the rest of the trip.

Captain Parker carefully read his maps for clarification and position. It would be his last voyage. He had made three trips with a heavy heart, so he wanted to take what he had and go ashore to live. The young slave boy, his mother, and the neighbor had been a big help on this last voyage. In his mind he had pondered on the fate of the three; what could he do to change the outcome? There was a commonest over Captain Parker. For some time, he dreaded what was to come, but three slaves now were tied into his future, and he wanted to do what he thought his heart was telling him. He could not undue what had happen in the past, and he could not start anew. He would save them and no longer deal in the selling of human beings. He looked back at his lodge. There would have to be some changes made in his paper work. The plain was to show that three extra slaves were lost at sea due to sickness or washed overboard in a storm. He would take them with him and give them a new life in a country where most of their kind was slaves; that's the least he could do to atone for his past action against humanity.

The Isadora was on its third trip to the Americas from Africa; which also would be its last voyage, as the contract was for three voyages to fill the quota needed for Mr. Collins' plantation. Captain Parker hoped that the nightmares would end. In the past year, the slave transport had not been easy, but he would be on shore starting a new life for himself while Jon, Ruby, and Hoppy would be lost to the slave world for ever without his help. His home would be a free home for all. The three slaves would live a life of freedom on the farm, but the rest of the world was not ready to accept slaves as equals. Captain made a vow that he would no longer participate. He had made his mistakes, and change was his only way to join the human race again. He was free; why shouldn't they be free too? For what was done to the oppressed, he could not change.

The captain glanced out over the ocean as he made his rounds taking time to talk to his crewmen on night watch. He wondered what it would be like to live on land. He had memories, but his life had been well spent on what he loved the most; being on the ocean. He reached back in his past when he was young and lived on the land; bits and pieces of his past could clearly be recalled, but somewhat distorted and events out of order. He tried hard to put the facts in the correct time frame but fail to do so. After a while his future plans and hopes took presence in his mind and what he would do once on land. The past memories did not dampen his new future plans. At that moment several of the deckhands spoke to the captain. "Ahoy Captain Parker!" one man said with a nod, and other crew members responded also with a nod. The captain responded with a peck on his hat brim. It was getting late and dark. As night filled the sky, Captain Parker made his way back to his cabin. When the captain entered his quarters, Jon had just prepared his bed for sleep, Ruby had laid out his clothes for bed, and Hoppy had filled his basin with warm water; his table set for dinner. The old gray head man would spend a quiet evening in his quarters. He sat before his table and food with a bottle of his favorite wine. He said grace, like he always does, then ate his food and drunk his wine, raising his head between bites looking out the window nearest him. It was a clear night; he could see the stars. He thought long about his future and what he could do. A sound came from the upper deck; the sound followed a particular cadence in its rhythms. It was some kind of string instrument; the musical sound flowed on the air faintly heard but enjoyed by all who heard it; creating a somber mood with each note played.

For a time, the night seem to part; giving way to the music, reminding its listeners of past events and then changing to an up tempo, making its listeners do a jiggle to the rhythms. It faded to nothing, disappearing into the night, like a ghost. In time the stillness, the darkness all relevant of the events appeared as if none of the moments were real; a figment of someone's imagination. Below deck all was quiet and all hopes wished for a better day. The accursed deal that had been struck months ago held everyone involved in a deadly grip. There was no turning back, the bargain had been made and the deal had to be carried out to the bitter end.

It was the captain, crew, and their dark prisoners below, all due to suffer. No good would ever come of this. Slavery was a bitter pill for all below deck and above. The Isadora had made her way to her first docking since departing from the dark coast. She now sits off the coast of South America in Para. She had completed half of her voyage. The ship's doctor, cook, first mate Rum 'dose met in the captain's quarters to receive their orders and also to give their reports of the day. Only nine of the precious cargo had been lost; mainly poor health, sickness, disease which was common in long voyages, and the close quarters of mixed groups of people put together without any medical history. Many of the natives who had died were weak or sick before their capture and the trauma of the ordeal of being made a captive killed them.

Para, South America would only be a stop for supplies. At this stage of the trip, fresh water and food was the main concern. They would only dock long enough for these provisions; just a day and a half giving the crew time to load and store the goods, clean the lower deck before putting out to sea once again. The ocean crossing in the open sea had come to an end. From here on out, land would be in reach. As they travel up the coast line of South America to North America; Havana and Cuba would be the next ports of call before sailing on to Mobile Alabama. As the supplies were placed on board, Rum 'dose did his head count to make sure all were aboard before they set sail on the evening tide. The slaves near the opening looked up at the large figured man who now stood just above them. The man gave the order. Everything was secure and the ship made its way back out to sea.

A stone-cold expression on the man's face did not change or show any form of compassion as he looked down at the captives to give his orders barking in a very demanding voice to the crew members. His eyes moved from one end of the platform where he stood, to the other. As the ship moved along the water-path which would lead to the next docking point, he looked toward what would be the shore; not seeing a sign of land, the crew now stood gazing at the tall figured man with anticipation of his next order to be carried out; without challenge. He turns toward the great wheel that stirred the ship where the captain stood in silence. The man's voice replied in each detail what had transpired in order, to the waiting commander. The captain replied back with a simple nod. The young black boy, Jon, and Ruby, and Hoppy could all be seen moving about in the galley looking up from time to time out on the deck which was now covered by darkness. The chores in time had been completed and they soon lay quietly on the galley's floor falling asleep with chains placed on their legs till morning. The three lay huddle together to keep warm from the air that blew through the partially opened door.

The Isadora had docked in Havana's waters late in the night. There would be no long boats to shore till morning and then the last supplies needed to complete the voyage to the Americas would be gathered and brought on board to hasten the departure. By noon the task of loading the goods were finished, and the vessel was put out to sea once more. All aboard appeared weary from the voyage; three crew members who were confined to the sleeping quarters from scurvy, and at least 20 of the cargo was sick from varies things, but there was still some ways to go. The ship's crew settled into their duties to pass the time. The weariness was a part of three long voyages across the ocean; within a day and a half, the ship would pull into port Mobile Alabama. Late that evening, they would cross the Gulf waters into the harbor area of Mobile. All members of the crew knew what that meant, but none of the cargo passengers knew anything about their home, their future, the new land they had been brought to in the dead of night.

The first part of the captive movement was now ending. New rules and regulation would be imposed. The captives were slaves who now belong to someone; much would be expected of them in their new home, and the only rights they had would be limited. All slept quietly above and below deck. Captain Parker sat at his desk with a cup of Ale in his hand staring blankly at the wall across from him. His life could also be changed in 48 hours. His heart was heavy; a life time had passed before him, and he did not recognize where it all started and where it would end. He still loved the sea, so it would be in his best interest to stay somewhere close to the shoreline. He did not care for Mobile. It was crowded with people, and It was just a small fishing village on the coast. He had found a patch of land a few miles outside the city limits that he could afford to pay. The land was just 30 acres; a small house and barn were the two buildings on the property. Parker knew the size of the house and the amount of land would be just what he and his three guests would need to start their new life on shore. Jon, Ruby and Hoppy would have a life in the new world without chains. He would see to that.

From Para, South America, the ship made its way north into the shipping lands of Havana and Cuba where they docked once more; only staying a half day and then on to the Gulf of Mexico passing up the Florida Keys. Moving west following the coastal shoreline; would take them to the port of Mobile Bay.

On December 22nd the year of our Lord, the Isadora entered the docking area of Mobile, Alabama just before sun rise. The city had not yet stirred and there was no one to greet her or her crew and passengers. The shoreline would be filled with on-lookers inspecting the new cargo from faraway places. The Americas offered a new life in a new country to all who came. This freedom was not a part of the slave trade. Whoever entered this place as a slave remains a slave with no rights or control of their future. However, the well-to-do had rights

As the day progressed Mr. Collins and his farm-hands made their way to the shore where the Isadora sat quietly off shore until the business at hand was completed for goods and slaves. Cargo and slaves were transferred to the holding area. By night-fall the forced march had started for the plantation which would be twenty or more miles in the first day. The group took its first break which lasted overnight, and when the sun rose the next day, the march began again. The full march to the plantation would take at least two and a half days depending on the slaves that were worst off, hindering the march from moving at a faster pace.

At this time the slave numbers was about 197. The voyage across the sea took the other 13 who died at sea. Jon, Ruby, and Hoppy were listed among the dead. That day the caravan left for the Collins Plantation. Captain Parker sold the Isadora, paid off his outstanding debts, and bought the small farm not far from the bay in Point-Clear the south tip of Alabama.

He bought his needed supplies for the new farm along with a wagon, two horses, a cow, ten chickens, two pigs and a goat. He began his quarter hour trip to the homestead. Ruby and Hoppy sat in the back of the wagon while Mr. Parker and Little Jon sat in the front seat to help steer the horses. Three black slaves and a white man now moved toward a new beginning, a new life, in a new land as a family. There would be many objections to the living arrangement. The life style that was contrary to new life in the new world. The three blacks had much to learn about their new home and Parker had much to teach his new family. One of the first big changes would be, No chains for his new family. They were free to move around without restriction on the property. They would learn to depend on each other even more as a family. Little Jon, Ruby, and Hoppy had been brought to America as slaves, and given their freedom and their names like all free souls with rights and freedom. Jon Parks, Ruby Parks, and Hoppy Parkson—others of their kind had not been so lucky. Physical abuse, sickness, and death had claimed many of their brothering on the voyage of the Isadora, and other slave ships bound for the Americas. Slavery was a business.

It made money for people who dealt in the enslavement of humans, but Jon, Ruby, and Hoppy had a new start. They were slaves for only 56 days and were freed by the very man who enslaved them.

Point Clear sat off on one of the main roads of the area, and the small road that lead to the farm was just beyond. The wagon made its way down to the house that sat on the left with two large trees blocking the view that exposed the farm house. Just behind the house was the barn, not very big, but it would serve the purpose it was needed for. The broken down picket fence surrounded three sides of the entrance to the estate giving land scape scenery to what was theirs. The barn also had its confinements too. One side of the building was shaded by a large tree and the other was a fence to corral a small group of animals if needed. There, two horses and a cow would be kept. The goat would roam free on the property.

The wagon stopped at the front door and all four of the riders disembarked and proceeded up the steps to the front door of the house. They would call this place home. Mr. Parker opened the door exposing the inside of the building. The dusty room looked like it had not been exposed to the outside world for some time. A thin layer of dirt covered the walls, floor, and the few furnishings. It would take some effort to clean and repair the sight for living, but this was home. Just above where they stood appeared a hole in the roof which needed immediate attention. Within a few days, Mr. Parker helped each new family member choose a first and last name to be referred to. Little Jon would be call Jon Parks and His mother would be Ruby Parks, and Hoppy was to be called Hoppy Parkson. All paper work from here on would bare all of their names as equal share holders. Slaves were not able to own property, but they were not slaves in the eyes of Jonathan Parker. It would take some time for the rest of the world to come to these ideas which would become the backbone of America's constitution. "All men was created equal"—they were a made up family, a family that was different than any other, but in many ways like any other family.

It was December 25th, Jonathan and Jon went out to gather fresh game for the table. It had taken most of the morning but the trip had been successful. They had 3 large pheasants; a turkey, 5 squirrels, and 2 rabbits; and an assortment of fruits and wild vegetables. When the meal had been completed they all sat around the table which had been built by the men of the group. Jonathan offered blessing in the form of a prayer to start the Christmas celebration.

Some miles away, the Collins plantation had finished their forced march home and they were starting their holiday feast. There were large groups of farm hands to be settled in their ranks of slaves. They were to be tagged and chained and then taken to a place where they would be housed, feed and given a day's rest before being put to work. The living quarters were 4 large buildings where all the slaves were kept. The overseers were the only ones with small shacks; which were separate living arrangements from the general population.

The four large structures had just one door and two windows at each end. There was a pit in the middle of the building in which meals could be cooked and fires for heat. The pit was deep in the earth and a large pot and skillet was the cooking utensil for each hut. Mr. Collins had not seen his slaves since their arrival. He and his family prepared for the feast. It was held in the big house; some ways from where the slave encampment was. Today there would be extra for all. The slave-hands who were given charge over the populas would see to the feeding and housing of the newcomers; who were kept separate for the first day or so. Many smells flood down from the big-house kitchen to where the slaves were. Some were to the likes they had never smelled before, which could be over whelming to a hungry man. The meats, the breads, the sweets, the many vegetables simmers in the area where they were cooking, ready to be taken to the table to be served to the host and his guest. As the day passed into the morning, through the afternoon, and into the evening; the festivities went on. The fine music could be heard throughout the estate. There was much laughter, singing and merry making to celebrate Christmas. There were many gifts exchanged between the people, and staff.

The slaves were given a day of rest and extra food. There would be no celebration for them. Tomorrow they would be back to work in the fields for most of the day. Down the road at the Parker's residence, each member of the new family had been assign quarters. Ruby and Hoppy shared a room with a door for privacy, Jonathan was down at the end of the hall in his room, and Lil Jon was given a small loft area which gave the young boy his privacy too.

On December 24th three ankle bracelets were removed and each was given their freedom for the first time. They were given a grand tour of the farm which would be their new home. One of the first words they were taught was "freedom" and its meaning... Free to go as you please. In time the English language would be their tongue too; they would learn to read and write like all free men and women in America. From this time on Christmas would have a special meaning to the house hold beyond celebrating the birth of Chris the Lord and Savior.

Two years had passed since Jonathan Parker had come ashore, bought a farm, started a family, and gave up the sea. He was a land dweller now, but the ocean would always be a part of him. Often times he would make pilgrimage to the sea.

To see the water, hear it beat against the shoreline. To smell the salt water was relaxing to him; It simple brought peace to the aging man who had made the water home for many years. Time ashore was making his trips less frequent, and the old memories' was starting to fade and replaced with better ones of his new life at the farm.

Soon it would be Christmas once again. Jonathan and Jon had risen early that morning, for they would have to hunt game for the table. The women of the house had been at the cooking at least an hour when the two men left out for the hunt; taking only jerky and water, for they would be gone for most of the day. Hoppy would work with the animals feeding which ever ones who had to be fed and put out to pasture and then return to help in the kitchen. Within two years, one lonely man and three slaves became a family; living in the same house, sharing a dwelling, working to become productive citizens no matter what the rest of the world responded to. There were no feelings of hate, and no attention given to color. Distrust was left at the door; only love and respect was given to all.

One had been the master, three had been slaves, but all had changed. Jonathan Parker carved out in his world on that small piece of land a new future of freedom. It would take others many years to reach his mild stone. It was a cold December day as Jonathan and Jon made their way deep in the woods tracking wild game for the feast; so far 2 rabbits, a squirrel had been trapped and 4 nice size fish had been the morning prize. This season hunting had been scarce due to the bad weather, unlike Africa, where the hunt was good most days because of the abundance of game found there. The bird which was to line the table topping of the meal was nowhere to be found. The American turkey was not easily caught, but tomorrow was another day to hunt. If this fails, they would eat chicken fresh from the yard.

The sun had all but set when Jonathan and Jon reached the farm with their game from the hunt. It would take some time to prepare the animals to be cooked. All of the family joins in to complete the task at hand. Ruby and Hoppy was very adapt to cooking in a kitchen and knew very well how to use the cooking utensils to prepare a meal. It was a happy time and they all thanked the creator for the life they now had. A time was set aside to pray for the unfortunate ones who knew nothing of freedom. Jonathan Parker stepped to the window that over looked the small farm. He knew he had done the right thing when he freed Jon, Ruby, and Hoppy. He wondered how long it will take the Americas to do the same.

There was a storm brewing out of the north. Land further north and northwest was already covered with 3 feet of snow which meant that it would be a white Christmas in the Americas. Once the weather reached further south, it would become wind with drenching rain. At the latest, the sun went behind the lowest hill in the west, and a thin mist began falling covering the land and the people. Jonathan Parker and his family was tucked safe inside their home. He thanked God for his new life and the will to give freedom to three special people, who meant a lot to him, and who helped him redeem himself. Thinking to himself, he wondered if the veil of slavery would be lifted and freedom would be given in the Americas and shown to all who made a home in this new land of freedom. The light that exited the Parker's house was a start. Let freedom ring, Let freedom ring for all!

THE END

www.ingramcontent.com/pod-product-compliance
Lightning Source LLC
Chambersburg PA
CBHW050919120626
46552CB00004B/1663